M.G. 22110

CHASING THE SHADOW

by Hubert Ben Kemoun

illustrated by Thomas Ehretsmann

translated by Genevieve Chamberland

Librarian Reviewer
Marci Peschke
Librarian, Dallas Independent School District
MA Education Reading Specialist, Stephen F. Austin State University
Learning Resources Endorsement, Texas Women's University

Reading Consultant
Elizabeth Stedem
Educator/Consultant, Colorado Springs, CO
MA in Elementary Education, University of Denver, CO

STONE ARCH BOOKS
MINNEAPOLIS   SAN DIEGO

First published in the United States in 2008
by Stone Arch Books,
151 Good Counsel Drive, P.O. Box 669
Mankato, Minnesota 56002
www.stonearchbooks.com

Library of Congress Cataloging-in-Publication Data
Ben Kemoun, Hubert, 1958–
    [Chasse à l'ombre. English]
    Chasing the Shadow / by Hubert Ben Kemoun; translated by Genevieve
Chamberland; illustrated by Thomas Ehretsmann.
    p. cm. — (Pathway Books Editions / The Adventures of Sam X)
    ISBN 978-1-4342-0478-3 (library binding)
ISBN 978-1-4342-0528-5 (paperback)
    [1. Shadows—Fiction. 2. Supernatural—Fiction.] I. Chamberland,
Genevieve. II. Ehretsmann, Thomas, ill. III. Title.
PZ7.B4248Ch 2008
[Fic]—dc22   2007030729

Summary: After Sam and his friend Lionel explore an old mine, Sam's
shadow disappears. It's difficult to be shadowless, so Sam and Lionel
return to the mine to try to find out where the shadow has gone.

Art Director: Heather Kindseth
Graphic Designer: Kay Fraser

1 2 3 4 5 6 13 12 11 10 09 08

TABLE OF CONTENTS

Chapter 1

UNDER THE SUN

"It's closed! Sam, don't tell me we rode all the way down here for nothing!" said my best friend, Lionel.

Lionel was perched on his bike, looking at a heavy steel door. The door was covered with barbed wire.

Lionel was covered with sweat. The two of us had been riding our bikes for over an hour in the hot sun. I crossed my arms.

"Of course it's closed!" I said. "This factory was shut down years ago. When our parents were kids."

I sighed. Then I went on, "What did you think? Did you think that we would drive up, push open the door, and go on a tour? People don't come here anymore. This place is empty. We're not on a field trip, Lionel. We're on an adventure!"

Lionel wiped the sweat from his forehead. "It's so hot out," he complained. "Why did you make me come all the way down here, instead of going swimming in the river?" Lionel frowned. He looked mad.

"It's not that bad," I said.

"This heat is killing me!" exclaimed Lionel. "We biked for six miles, and it's got to be 100 degrees out! We should have gone swimming at the river, Sam. It was really stupid to come here."

"An old, empty glass factory is way more fun than the river," I said. "There's no one here but us. Isn't this cool?"

Lionel snorted. "Ha! Cool is the one thing it's not," he said. He was still frowning.

Lionel sat down in the shade under a tree. He looked really mad, and he was sweating a lot.

"You're so boring, Lionel," I told him. "This is supposed to be an adventure."

It was our last chance to have an adventure at the old glass factory. It was supposed to be torn down in a month. The city council had decided to build a big amusement park where the factory had been. If we wanted to explore the glass factory, today was the day.

I looked around. I wanted to get closer to the factory. "Come on," I said. "There must be some way to get inside. Let's leave our bikes here and walk around back to look."

"Fine," said Lionel. "But I'm walking in the shade."

I rolled my eyes. I was hot too, but weekends were for exploring!

We walked in the shade next to the building. Lionel was behind me.

In the back of the old factory, the wall had caved in. It left a gap about three feet wide. It was just big enough for us to climb through.

"Once we cross those burning stones, we will be inside the ancient fortress," I told Lionel.

"Burning stones?" asked Lionel. "Fortress?" He laughed. "You're crazy," he told me.

"Oh, come on, Lionel," I said. "No one else is here. We can claim this land as our own kingdom. We are the kings of the world!"

Inside the wall was an empty, dusty yard. At one end of the yard were a few old sheds. In the middle of the yard, blazing in the afternoon sun, was a mound of dirt that was 30 feet high.

"Wow!" said Lionel. For once, he didn't look mad.

"This is like the Sahara desert," I said.

"Yeah," said Lionel. "It even has a big pile of sand in the middle!"

"That's not sand," I said. "It's clay. My mom told me about it. It's the kind of clay that they use to make stuff like plates and cups. And what's really cool is that I heard that this glass factory is built over a mine."

Lionel didn't look like he cared. "Who cares? I'm burning up. Let's go home," he said with a sigh. "My mom bought ice cream at the store yesterday. We can have some!"

I had to admit, Lionel was sweating a lot. And ice cream did sound good.

"Here, take this," I said, handing him my water bottle. Lionel took a big drink.

"You can have the rest," I told him. "Then we'll leave."

"Great!" said Lionel. "Let's get out of here."

"After we find the mine and go exploring," I added.

"What? Well, okay," Lionel said. "At least it won't be so hot inside the mine."

Chapter 2

UNDERGROUND

First, we explored the factory. We were trying to find the entrance to the mine. The factory was empty and most of the roof was caved in.

We had to watch where we stepped because the floor was covered with broken glass. We could see large ovens for making pottery, some old wood shelves, and a bunch of old, rusty tools. Some of it was cool stuff.

The place was full of dust, mice, and dirt. There wasn't much else there.

I was about to tell Lionel that he was right. There was nothing there. We should head back home.

Then I saw it.

Finally. I'd found the entrance to the mine.

It was a little shed next to the main building. The door was locked with a huge metal padlock.

I turned to Lionel. "Look!" I said. "These tracks look like railroad tracks. I bet that door is where the carts went down into the mine."

"So what?" he asked. "There's no way in. The door is locked. Come on, Sam. We tried. Now let's just go home, before we die from the heat!"

I didn't pay attention to him. I pretended like I hadn't heard. Then I tried to open the rusty old door. Like I told Lionel, it's not an adventure if it's too easy!

The rusty lock was so old that it fell apart. I pulled the heavy door open.

"I don't like this!" Lionel said. He crossed his arms. I was really starting to get tired of Lionel. He kept wrecking my adventure.

"I'll go first," I said. "You can have the flashlight if you want. We'll come right back up. I promise."

Lionel didn't say anything. He just grabbed the flashlight.

Then we walked inside the mine. Lionel stayed close behind me. We followed the old railroad tracks down a steep tunnel of gray rock.

"See?" I said. "It's nice and cool down here."

Lionel didn't say anything. He was holding the flashlight right behind me. The light made my shadow stretch far out in front of us. My shadow looked really gigantic as it bounced around on the wall.

After about ten minutes, we came to a huge, round cave. Four tunnels came together to form the cave.

In the cave, four empty metal carts stood next to a pile of shovels, picks, and rusty iron buckets.

"This place is as big as a football stadium," I said, impressed. The cave echoed when I spoke.

Then I saw something.

"Point the light on that wall over there," I told Lionel. "It looks like there's something written on the wall."

"Brrr! I'm getting cold," said Lionel, shivering.

I rolled my eyes. "Just shine the light on the wall," I told him.

He shone the flashlight on the wall.

Words had been carved into the rock. They were messages that had been left behind by the former miners.

"I'm thirsty," I said. Lionel handed me the water bottle. I finished it and tossed it aside. Then I read the messages out loud. My voice echoed through the huge cave.

Here I sweated for fifteen years.
Barnaby
Farewell to you, mine! I hated you as
much as I loved you. Carter
We were here. Obie

"Okay," said Lionel. "That's good enough for me. We came down here and we saw stuff. Now let's get out of here!"

I was still looking at the cave wall. I wanted to read more names, dates, and farewell notes that the miners had written down.

There were hundreds of messages. The wall was covered with their writing. It was pretty cool.

"I'm going home, Sam," said Lionel. He turned to walk away.

Just then, I had an idea. I knew what I had to do.

"Wait a minute," I said. "We need to leave a message on the wall too. I mean, we were here, just like the miners were, right?"

I picked up a big iron nail from the
ground. Using the sharp end of the nail, I
carved my message in the rock.

Barnaby is not the only one
who sweated here.

Sam and Lionel, the last visitors!

"Whatever," said Lionel. He sounded mad again.

He turned around, still holding the flashlight. I was suddenly covered in deep darkness.

"Hey!" I shouted. "Bring back the flashlight!"

I ran toward Lionel and I tripped over one of the iron buckets. It rolled and banged on the floor. It echoed so loud that I was scared. It sounded like the whole cave was making noise.

"Wait for me!" I yelled. But Lionel wasn't waiting.

I finally caught up with him halfway up the tunnel. He was still mad when we got to our bicycles, waiting outside the factory.

He didn't say anything. He just hopped on his bike and started pedaling.

I jumped on my bike too, and hurried to catch up.

The ride back home was even hotter than the ride to the factory had been. The afternoon sun blazed down on us.

Our shadows stretched out ahead of us on the flat road.

At least that's what I thought.

After we had gone about a mile, Lionel, who was riding behind me, let out a scream. "Sam!" he yelled.

I slammed my foot down on the side of the hot road. "What?" I yelled back.

"Sam!" he cried. "Look down at the ground!"

I looked at the ground. There was nothing there.

"What? What's wrong?" I asked, gazing at the street.

"Your shadow!" he said.

"What about my shadow?" I said.

Then I saw it. Or, I mean, I didn't see it. My shadow was gone!

I couldn't believe it. There was Lionel's shadow. There were the shadows from our bikes.

There was nothing where my shadow should have been.

Chapter 3

SHADOWLESS

Someone who loses their sight is called blind. Someone who loses their hearing is called deaf.

What do you call someone who loses their shadow?

There isn't a word for it, because nobody ever loses their shadow. It has never happened to anyone, ever before. No one has ever lost their shadow.

Except me.

I searched on the road for it. I dropped off Lionel at his house, because he was really freaked out, and then I searched some more. Then I went home, searching the whole time. I still didn't have a shadow.

No big deal, I told myself. Who needs a shadow? What does a shadow do for you anyway?

Besides, I thought, no one would notice that my shadow was missing. Why would they? No one ever looks at anyone's shadow.

It was summer. The sun was really bright. Would someone see that my shadow was gone?

That night, I was lying on my bed with the lights turned off. When I turned on my bedside lamp, I tried to make shadow animals on the wall.

It was no use. My shadow was gone. Would it ever come back?

I couldn't make birds or monsters or robots. I used to be so good at making shadow animals with my hands.

That was before the cave!

Was that why all of this was happening? Was it because I went down into that mine?

I didn't understand. Everything was getting stranger and stranger.

I hoped that the next day, my shadow would be back. Maybe a good night's sleep would help.

Then my mom stuck her head into my bedroom. "What are you doing in the dark?" she asked. She reached toward the light switch.

"Don't turn on the light!" I said. "I feel sick. The light is hurting my eyes."

I was sure that if anyone would notice that my shadow was missing, it would be my mom.

"Too much biking in the hot sun,"
she said. My mom smiled at me. "Come
to dinner," she said, "and then you can
go right back to bed. You need a good
night's sleep so you're ready for your big
game tomorrow."

Oh no! We had a basketball game the
next day! And I was the star player on
the fourth-grade team.

The game would be held after school. We'd be playing outside, on the basketball courts. In the full, bright sun. Everyone else's shadows would be there.

* * *

The next morning, Lionel was waiting for me at school. "Your shadow is still missing!" he exclaimed as I walked up.

"Gee, Lionel, tell the whole school," I said. "If you want to talk, let's talk in the shade."

We walked to a corner, where no one would notice my missing shadow.

"I've been thinking," Lionel said quietly. "I'm pretty sure this shadow thing is because you went into the mine. But I can't figure out why it didn't happen to me. It's not normal!"

"Not normal?" I said. "Of course it's not normal. Nothing about me is normal anymore."

"Calm down, Sam. You're still the same," Lionel said, smiling.

Then he paused. "Except for one small, weird thing, of course," he added.

He was trying to make me feel better, but it really wasn't helping. I just sighed.

Then Lionel said, "I still have your flashlight. We should go back down the mine tonight."

"Don't think about tonight. Keep your minds on today!" said a grown-up voice. It was our principal, Mr. Blister.

Mr. Blister said, "So, are you two coming to school today, or are you going to stand there and hold up the building? It's not quite summer vacation yet, you know."

Every morning, Mr. Blister made sure every single student entered the school on time. I don't know if he ever did anything else.

Lionel and I walked along the side of the building in the shade, where the sun wasn't shining.

In class, I switched desks with Lionel so that I could be farther from the window. I told my teacher that I had just found out I was allergic to sunlight. I don't think she believed me, but she let me stay where I was.

As the day went on, I kept looking at other people's shadows. Their shadows on the floor grew shorter and shorter as the morning passed by. I was jealous of their shadows!

I was afraid a student would yell, "Look, there's something weird about Sam. Look at the floor!" Luckily, that didn't happen.

During recess, I was careful to stay in the shade. But after lunch, I started getting really worried about the basketball game.

How could I avoid being noticed during the game? I was the team's best player. If I stayed on the bench, in the shade, people would know that something was going on.

I was still nervous after school. The game was about to start. I took a deep breath and walked out onto the court.

It was awful. Everyone's shadows were dark and clear on the concrete court. All of the shadows, that is, except one.

Every time I had the ball, I was worried that people were staring at me. I moved around the court as fast as I could.

If I stayed close to the other players, their shadows would be close too. Then nobody would notice that mine wasn't there.

After ten minutes and eight baskets, I was dripping with sweat. I was starting to feel better. No one had noticed my missing shadow yet.

Then something awful happened.

"Sam!" my teammate Paul called. "Sam," he said, "you don't have a shadow!"

"Pass the ball!" I said.

"No really, I mean it. Look!" Paul yelled.

Lionel saw what was happening. He quickly ran over. "Don't say anything," he said to Paul. "It's a secret. Sam is part of a special experiment at the hospital. An experiment to fight sweat. It could change everything. Sweaty people would start to smell good."

"It doesn't seem to be working very well," Paul pointed out.

I wiped my face on my shirt. It was really hot out!

"The doctor warned me it could take a while to work. Also, the medicine might make me do weird things," I told Paul. "When my shadow comes back, I might start drooling and biting!"

"He's not kidding," whispered Lionel. "You should see the scar I have on my shoulder!"

"Um, let's get back to the game," said Paul. He ran away quickly, with a scared look on his face.

"Thanks, Lionel," I said.

I hoped Lionel's story would make Paul stop wondering about my shadow, but it didn't. Before the end of the game, the whole team knew about my sweat experiment.

In the locker room, Max came over to my locker and stood right in front of me. "I don't believe that story about your shadow," he said.

"You're right," I said. "The truth is, I forgot my shadow on the clothesline this morning."

Max looked confused. "What do you mean?" he asked.

"You mean you never wash yours?" I asked. "Gross!"

Max's mouth fell open. All the other boys laughed.

"Very funny," Max said. Then he turned and walked out of the locker room.

Great, I thought. If Max told the whole school, my secret would be out.

But it turned out that I didn't have anything to worry about. When Lionel and I came out of the locker room, the sky was dark and a terrible storm had already started.

I don't know if Max told anyone what I had said, but no one else mentioned my shadow for the rest of the day. That was a relief.

That afternoon, in the pouring rain,
Lionel and I biked six miles back to the
old mine.

Chapter 4

THE HUNT

Water was running down the railroad tracks. A muddy stream was flowing into the mine.

I don't know how many times Lionel and I tripped and slipped. We followed the tracks into the tunnel.

Wet and tired, we finally reached the gigantic underground cave. A large puddle of muddy water was covering the entire floor.

"What are we looking for?" asked Lionel, waving the flashlight on the dark puddle.

"I don't know," I answered. "This is where my shadow disappeared, so maybe this is where I can get it back. Over there is the writing on the wall. And there's the bucket I tripped on when I was running back to you. Maybe when I tripped, the bucket made something happen."

I looked at Lionel. Then I saw his face freeze.

"Your shadow didn't disappear, Sam!" he whispered. He raised his hand and pointed at one of the rock walls. "Look!" he said.

What a shock! I felt like someone had punched me in the face.

There, a few feet away, was my shadow. It was alive, moving along the rocky wall, as if it were another person.

Was it really my shadow? It was shaped like me, but how could I tell if it was mine?

I ran toward it. Just as I was about to touch it, the shadow jumped to the side and escaped me.

It's a weird feeling to chase your own shadow. I couldn't grab it. My shadow was really fast.

The water in the cave was rising higher and higher. Before long, it was up to my waist. A bucket floated past me.

"Maybe we need to put the bucket back where it was," I said. "Remember the bucket that I kicked? Then maybe my shadow will come back to me."

"I don't think that's the problem," said Lionel. Besides, there were four buckets floating in the water. I didn't know which one I'd kicked.

"The water is getting higher," said Lionel. "We have to get out of here!"

My shadow was dancing on the wall. Outside, the storm was getting worse.

I stared at the walls, looking at all the messages from the old miners.

I looked carefully at the one I had written. Then I noticed a strange message. I hadn't seen it the day before.

IF YOU LEAVE SOMETHING IN THIS MINE,

YOU LEAVE A PART OF YOU BEHIND

I had left part of me behind all right. My shadow! But what had I left in the mine?

Then I realized. I had written my name on the wall!

"We have to erase our names!" I said. "This is all because I wrote on the wall!"

I ran toward the wall and scratched at our names with my fingernails.

The rock seemed harder than it had been the day before. My fingers started to hurt from scraping at the letters.

"We have to go," said Lionel. "The water's getting higher! It's better to live without a shadow than to drown down here with one!"

"Not yet!" I said. "I can still read the letters."

Lionel waved the flashlight in my face. I pushed him away.

"Sam, we really need to get above ground," he said. "We'll come back tomorrow, or the day after. I promise. But we have to get out of here before we drown. We have to go, right now. I mean it, Sam!"

I ignored him. I was getting tired from scrubbing, and my fingers were covered in blood. But I wouldn't stop. I couldn't stop.

Finally, my message was erased. I took a deep breath. But my shadow was still not back.

I was desperate. I turned toward the darkness. I know it sounds crazy, but I talked to my shadow.

"Please come back!" I begged. "I miss you. You're part of me. Come back and we can make shadow animals on my bedroom wall again. I'll even teach you new ones. Please, shadow, come back!"

You'll never guess what happened next. It was incredible!

My shadow answered me. "You forgot something, Samuel!" it said.

I shivered.

The shadow's voice, which sounded strangely like mine, shook the cave walls like thunder.

"What did I forget?" I asked.

"You erased what you should not have written," said my shadow. "That's good. But you forgot this."

My shadow was holding a water bottle. Lionel and I had brought it the day before. I had thrown it on the ground while we were reading the miners' old messages.

"This room holds the memories of those who worked hard, " added the shadow. "You treated this place as your own property. You used it as a garbage dump. Take your garbage out of here!"

I was shaking like a leaf. I took the bottle that my shadow handed me.

Then my shadow said, "And one more thing. If you had not come back with your friend, I would have been even angrier. I would have left you forever."

Lionel and I ran out of the cave, splashing through the muddy stream.

Once we passed through the mine door and left the old glass factory, the sun came out again. I noticed that my shadow was back.

It was right where it should be. It moved perfectly with my own movements.

* * *

Well, not really perfectly.

During the next week, whenever Lionel and I rode our bikes near the factory, my shadow left me for a while.

I can guess where it went. It went down into the mine.

The mine is closed up now, because the factory was torn down. No one can ever go back down there again.

I think my shadow visits that large underground cave whenever it can. I think it remembers how it ran free for a summer day.

Down there, for a few minutes, the shadow is in his own world, not mine.

THE END

ABOUT THE AUTHOR

Hubert Ben Kemoun was born in 1958 in Algeria, on the northern coast of Africa. He has written plays for radio, screenplays for television, musicals for the stage, and children's books. He now lives in Nantes, France with his wife and their two sons, Nicolas and Nathan. He likes writing detective stories, and also creates crossword puzzles for newspapers. When he writes stories, he writes them first with a pen and then copies the words onto a computer. His favorite color is black, the color of ink.

ABOUT THE ILLUSTRATOR

Thomas Ehretsmann was born in 1974 on the eastern border of France in the town of Mulhouse (pronounced mee-yoo-looz). He created his own comic strips at the age of 6, inspired by the newspapers his father read. Ehretsmann studied decorative arts in the ancient cathedral town of Strassbourg, and worked with a world-famous publisher of graphic novels, Delcourt Editions. Ehretsmann now works primarily as an illustrator of books for adults and children.

GLOSSARY

adventure (ad-VEN-chur)—an exciting or dangerous experience

desperate (DESS-pur-it)—if you are desperate, you will do anything to change your situation

effort (EF-urt)—if you make an effort, you try hard

experiment (ek-SPER-uh-ment)—a test to see the effect of something

factory (FAK-tuh-ree)—a building where something is made, using machines

fortress (FOR-triss)—a place that is strong, to protect those inside from attack

mine (MINE)—an underground place where minerals are dug up. A person who works in a mine is called a **miner**.

normal (NOR-muhl)—usual or regular

territory (TER-uh-tor-ee)—the land under the control of one ruler

tunnel (TUHN-uhl)—a passage built underground

MORE ABOUT . . .

People have been interested in shadows for thousands of years. Many cultures have special beliefs about shadows. Here are just a few of them!

- A folktale in Arizona tells of a mysterious shadow train that rides across the desert — where there are no train tracks!

- In the book *Peter Pan* by J. M. Barrie, Peter keeps losing his shadow. His friend Wendy tries to help him by sewing the shadow onto his clothes.

- In ancient Egypt, people thought that if a person's shadow ever disappeared, the person would die. They thought a shadow contained a part of the person's life.

... Shadows!

- The ancient Chinese believed that if you ever met a person without a shadow, that person must be a ghost!

- The Yoruba people of Nigeria believe that when you die, your shadow waits for you to return.

- The most famous shadows belong to the special groundhogs who live in a town in Pennsylvania called Punxsutawney (pronounced punk-suh-TAW-ney). If the rodent named Punxsutawney Phil sees his shadow on February 2, Groundhog Day, there will be six more weeks of winter. If he does not see his shadow, spring will soon arrive.

DISCUSSION QUESTIONS

1. Why was Sam so upset that his shadow was gone?

2. Sam's shadow tells him that if Sam had come back without Lionel, the shadow would never have returned to him. What do you think that means?

3. Sam's friends notice that his shadow is gone during a basketball game outside. If you lost your shadow, what are some of the places you would avoid so that no one would notice that you were shadowless?

WRITING PROMPTS

1. Inside the mine, Sam and Lionel find messages from miners. Pretend that you're one of the miners. What message would you leave?

2. Sam says that there's no point to a weekend if you can't go exploring. What is your favorite thing to do on the weekend? Write about it!

3. Sam wants to pretend that he is the ruler of a grand territory (which is really just the mine and the factory). Have you ever used your imagination to create a territory of your own? Write about it, and draw a picture.

INTERNET SITES

Do you want to know more about subjects related to this book? Or are you interested in learning about other topics? Then check out FactHound, a fun, easy way to find Internet sites.

Our investigative staff has already sniffed out great sites for you!

Here's how to use FactHound:

1. Visit *www.facthound.com*

2. Select your grade level.

3. To learn more about subjects related to this book, type in the book's ISBN number: **9781434204783**.

4. Click the **Fetch It** button.

FactHound will fetch the best Internet sites for you!